The Misadventures of
SALEM HYDE

5

Frozen Fiasco
Frank Cammuso

AMULET BOOKS
NEW YORK

Hardcover ISBN: 978-1-4197-1651-5
Paperback ISBN: 978-1-4197-1652-2

Text and illustrations copyright © 2015 Frank Cammuso
Book design by Frank Cammuso and Alyssa Nassner

Published in 2015 by Amulet Books, an imprint of ABRAMS.

Printed and bound in China
10 9 8 7 6 5 4 3 2 1

Amulet Books are available at special discounts when purchased in quantity for premiums and promotions as well as fundraising or educational use. Special editions can also be created to specification. For details, contact specialsales@abramsbooks.com or the address below.

ABRAMS
THE ART OF BOOKS SINCE 1949

115 West 18th Street
New York, NY 10011
www.abramsbooks.com

4

6

7

8

13

14

16

21

24

25

26

39

40

42

46

50

59

63

70

72

84

89

SPECIAL THANKS TO . . .

Ngoc and Khai, Kathy Leonardo, Nancy Iacovelli, Nicole Sclama, Alyssa Nassner, Jim Armstrong, Elizabeth Peskin, Charlie Kochman, Chad Beckerman, Morgan Dubin, and Judy Hansen.

FOR MORE FUN STUFF ABOUT
SALEM AND WHAMMY
CHECK OUT MY WEBSITE AT . . .

WWW.CAMMUSO.COM

ALSO AVAILABLE

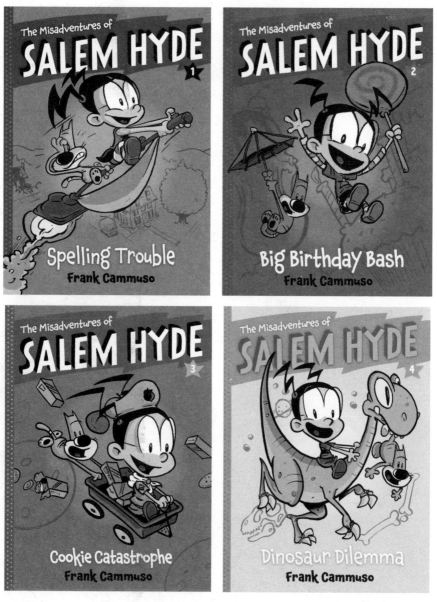